Fantastic Fairy Tales

# THE MAGIC PORRIDGE POT

An imprint of Om Books International

Once upon a time, there lived a girl named Lotte in a tiny little cottage at the end of the village. Lotte and her mother were very poor and her mother worked very hard to make ends meet.

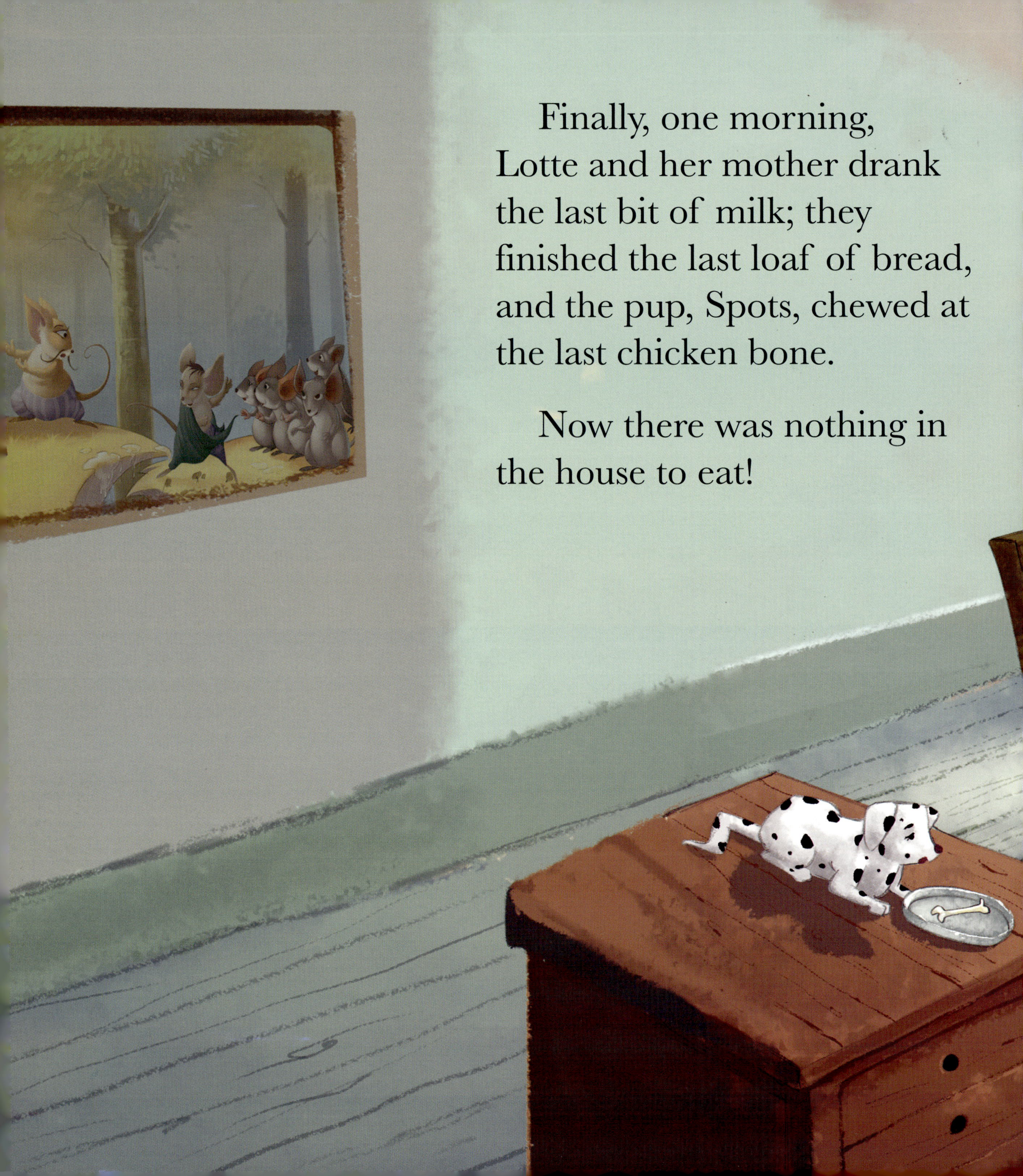

Finally, one morning, Lotte and her mother drank the last bit of milk; they finished the last loaf of bread, and the pup, Spots, chewed at the last chicken bone.

Now there was nothing in the house to eat!

"Run along to the woods, Lotte," said Mother, "and see if you can find some berries for us to eat."

Lotte's mother gave her a basket to bring back the berries in and Lotte skipped merrily to the woods with Spots. She loved to go to the green woods.

Once they reached the woods, Spots walked off, sniffing and digging at the ground.

Little Lotte looked high and low for berries, but couldn't find a single one! The shrubs had no berries, nor the trees - even the ground had none.

Disappointed, Lotte turned to go back home with her empty basket. Just then, a kind looking old lady appeared before her with a POOF!

"Why do you look so sad, little girl?" asked the old lady.

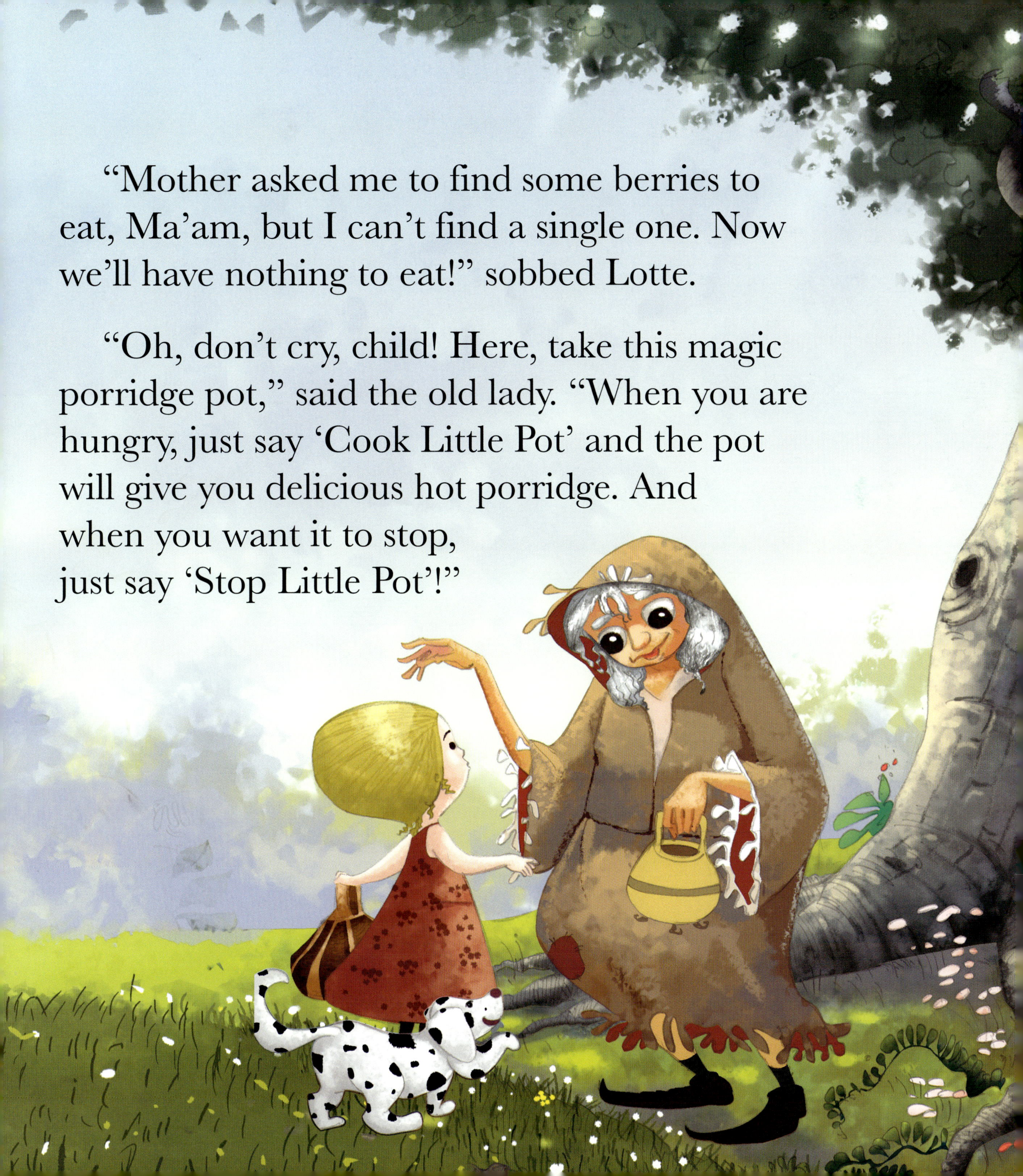

"Mother asked me to find some berries to eat, Ma'am, but I can't find a single one. Now we'll have nothing to eat!" sobbed Lotte.

"Oh, don't cry, child! Here, take this magic porridge pot," said the old lady. "When you are hungry, just say 'Cook Little Pot' and the pot will give you delicious hot porridge. And when you want it to stop, just say 'Stop Little Pot'!"

Lotte came back home happily, and told her mother about the strange old lady and the magic porridge pot that she had given her.

"Ah! What wonderful luck!" exclaimed Mother. "Let's eat supper now, Lotte."

"Cook Little Pot!" said Lotte, and the pot filled up with piping hot porridge.

When Mother, Lotte and Spots had eaten enough, "Stop Little Pot!" said Lotte.

Lotte and her mother were very happy and relieved now. They could eat healthy porridge any time they wanted to.

Next day, Lotte waved her mother goodbye and went out to play with her friends.

When it was time for lunch, Lotte had still not come back home. Now, Spots was very hungry and was running all around the house, barking and pulling at Mother's clothes, demanding porridge.

So Mother finally gave in. She picked up the magic porridge pot and placed it on the table.

"Cook Little Pot!" she said, and the pot filled up with porridge.

And then it began to overflow!

Mother had forgotten what to say to make the pot stop cooking. She tried everything she could.

"Stop Cooking!"

"Porridge Stop!"

"Stop Right Now!"

"Bad Cooking Pot!"

But nothing worked. The entire cottage was flooded with porridge right up to the roof. Mother and Spots ran out into the open and the porridge began to flow out from the windows and the doors of the cottage!

A huge river of porridge travelled down the streets of the village, reaching every nook and corner, every house, till all the people were swimming in it!

Finally, Lotte came and cried out, "Stop Little Pot!"

Mother, Spots and all the villagers sighed with relief as the pot stopped cooking. But what was to be done about the village? How would such a big place be cleaned?

Well, that was simple. It was lunch time, after all. So, everyone came out with their spoons and soon ate all the porridge.

What a delicious porridge feast for all!